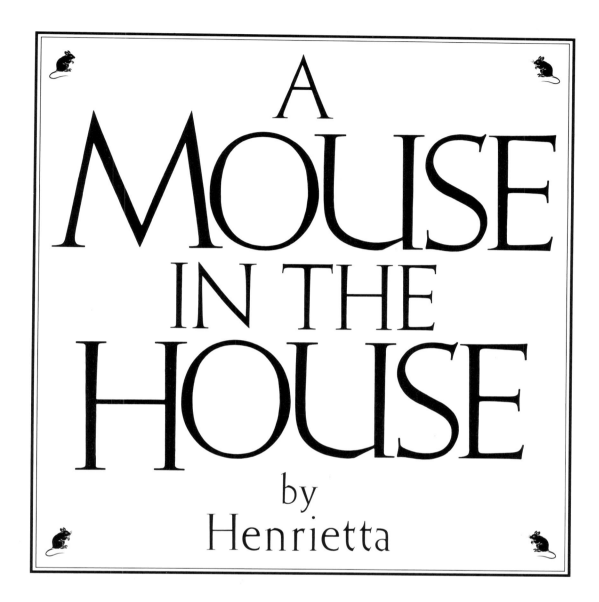

A MOUSE IN THE HOUSE

by
Henrietta

DK

DORLING KINDERSLEY

London • New York • Stuttgart

A DORLING KINDERSLEY BOOK

Managing Editor Jane Yorke
Editor Andrea Pinnington
Design by Mark Richards
Photography by Tim Ridley
Production Marguerite Fenn

Dorling Kindersley would like to thank Liz Button. David Corke.
Hilary Foster. Intellectual Animals. Christine Joslin. The Lighthouse.
Gatto Pavone. and Carolyn Russell for their help in producing this book.

First published in Great Britain in 1991
by Dorling Kindersley Limited.
9 Henrietta Street. London WC2E 8PS

A CIP catalogue record for this book is available from the British Library

ISBN 0-86318-693-9

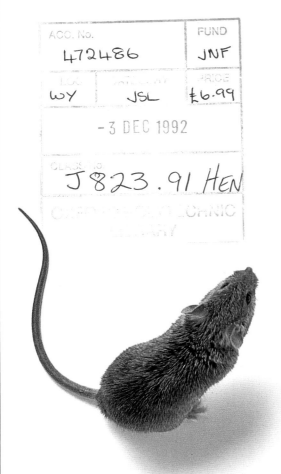

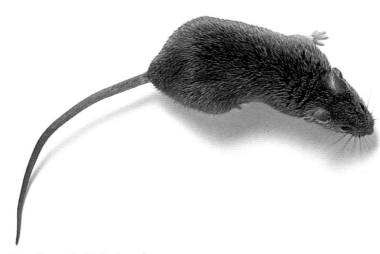

Typeset by The Graphic Unit. London
Reproduced in Italy by G.R.B. Graphica. Verona
Printed by Graphicom in Italy

*T*oday is a birthday! Today is a treat!
Some friends are invited to play and to eat.

*T*he house is all ready, balloons at the door,
But no one has seen me down here on the floor.

I wasn't invited, but I'll be a guest,
At this birthday party, along with the rest.

*O*n each page, in each room, I'll be doing my worst.
Can *you* find me hiding? Will cat find me first?

*T*here are lots of nice things that may look like a mouse,
But there's only one *me*, a *real* mouse in this house.

Garden room first, where I nibble my way
Through presents, well-hidden for this special day.

*K*itchen shelves next! There is coffee and tea,
And cheese left uncovered, just waiting for me.

Kitten-shaped biscuits, ready to bake,
A taste of the icing, now I'll try the cake!

12

Gifts in the hallway, coats in a heap,
I can hide safely while cat is asleep.

The party is swinging, the candles are blown,
But I've had a fabulous feast of my own!

*N*ow to the playroom to play with the toys,
But where are the girls? And where are the boys?

19

*N*o one is watching, so I'll just explore,
Oh dear! Teddy's stuffing has spilt on the floor!

There's a boat in the bathroom that I'd like to sail,
And now I'm all wet from my nose to my tail!

Night-time is coming, I'll soon go upstairs,
But first wait for Teddy to have his repairs.

On to the attic, the best is for last,
No one comes up, I can hide in the past.

26

CUNARD LINE

CLASS PASSENGER'S PER

FROM

SAILING DATE

ALBERGO MILANO

TRIESTE

WH

Puss w

Sl

27

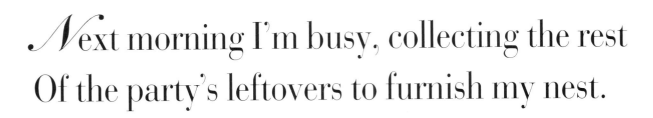

Next morning I'm busy, collecting the rest
Of the party's leftovers to furnish my nest.

I've explored every room to find every scrap,
And now that I'm finished, I'll stop for a nap.

I see paws at the door! The cat seeks a mouse.
I may have to move on — is there room in *your* house?